NO LONGER PROPERTY OF
KING COUNTY LIBRARY SYSTEM

FEB 2017

PRINCE RIBBIT

For Tony and Lisa – J. E.

For my children, my true princes – P. B.

Published by
PEACHTREE PUBLISHERS
1700 Chattahoochee Avenue
Atlanta, Georgia 30318-2112
www.peachtree-online.com

Text © 2016 Jonathan Emmett
Illustrations © 2016 Poly Bernatene

First published in Great Britain in 2016 by Macmillan Children's Books, an imprint
of Pan Macmillan, a division of Macmillan Publishers International Limited

First United States version published in 2017 by Peachtree Publishers

All rights reserved. No part of this publication may be reproduced, stored in
a retrieval system, or transmitted in any form or by any means—electronic,
mechanical, photocopy, recording, or any other—except for brief quotations in
printed reviews, without the prior permission of the publisher.

Illustrations were rendered digitally.

Printed in September 2016 by Shenzhen Wing King Tong Paper Products Co Ltd,
Guangdong, China
10 9 8 7 6 5 4 3 2 1
First Edition

ISBN 978-1-56145-761-8

Cataloging-in-Publication Data is available
from the Library of Congress.

Written by
Jonathan Emmett

Illustrated by
Poly Bernatene

PRINCE
RIBBIT

PEACHTREE
ATLANTA

KING COUNTY LIBRARY SYSTEM

"The Princess and the Frog Prince got married and lived happily ever after," read Princess Arabella, closing the book with a satisfied sigh.

Princess Lucinda frowned. "That silly girl treated the Frog Prince so badly! She was lucky he married her."

"If I ever met a talking frog, I wouldn't make the same mistake," agreed Arabella.

Princess Martha rolled her eyes. She liked facts more than fairy tales and real frogs more than enchanted ones. She'd heard a real frog croaking in the royal pond many times, but she could never spot him.

He's a clever little thing, thought Martha.

Martha was right. The frog was very clever, indeed. He often listened in on the sisters' stories, and the more he heard of princes and princesses, the more he longed to live like them.

The frog dreamed of sleeping in a soft bed, eating fine foods, and wearing a beautiful crown—and he'd just come up with a cunning plan to make his dream come true…

"EEEYUCK! Go away, you slimy little beast!" shrieked Arabella and Lucinda as the frog hopped out in front of them.

But the frog did not go away. Instead, he cleared his throat *and spoke.*

"Allow me to introduce myself," said the sly frog. "My name is Prince Ribbit."

Arabella and Lucinda stared, open mouthed, but Martha was delighted.

"It's a FROG," she shouted. "A TALKING FROG!"

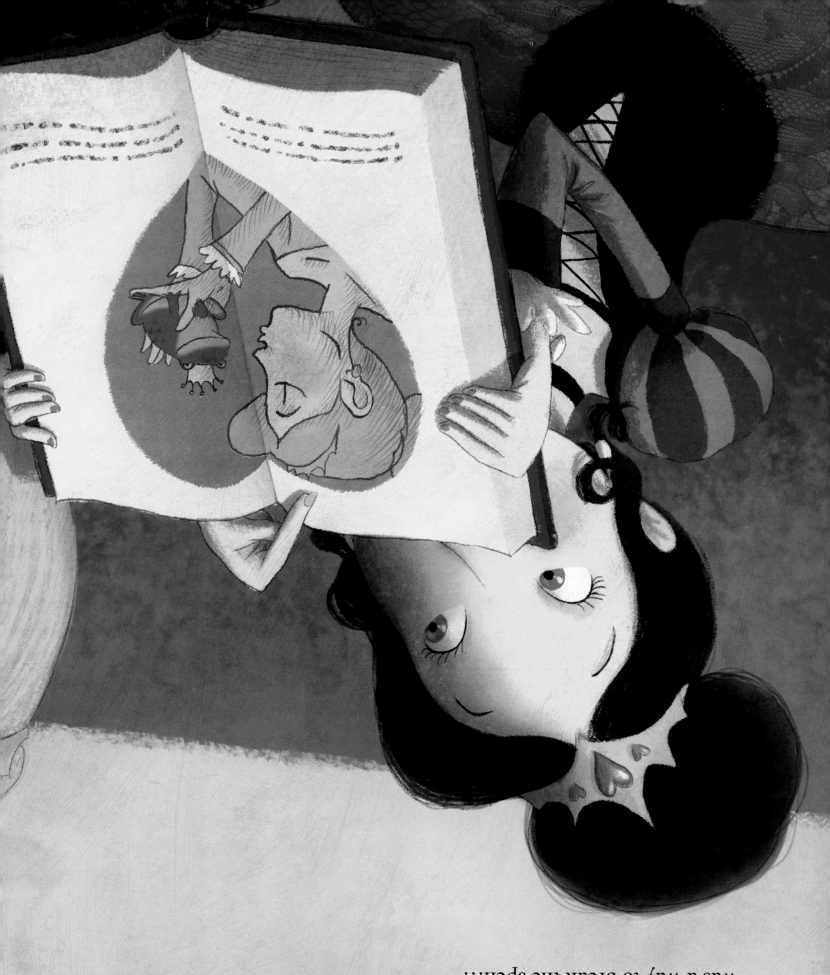

"Actually, I am an enchanted prince," he said. "A jealous wizard turned me into a frog because I was so astonishingly handsome! If only there was a way to break the spell..."

"But there is!" cried Lucinda. "It's in this book. You just need to be looked after by a pretty princess like me!"

"Or a pretty princess like *me!*" said Arabella. "And then you'll turn back into your old astonishingly handsome self, and we can live happily ever after!"

...while Arabella let him
eat from her plate.

Lucinda let him
sleep on her pillow...

Lucinda and Arabella took Prince Ribbit
back to the palace and gave him whatever he wanted.

But the more Princess Martha saw of the frog, the more suspicious she became.

"Why are you making such a fuss of him?" she asked as Prince Ribbit hopped around the dinner table.

"Because he's an enchanted prince," said Arabella, "and that's how you break the spell!"

"Just because it's in a book doesn't mean it's true," said Martha.

And with that, she went to the royal library to look up the truth about frogs.

"A mother frog lays eggs," she explained to her sisters. "Then the eggs turn into tadpoles, and the tadpoles turn into frogs. But frogs don't EVER turn into princes!"

"Just because it's in a book doesn't mean it's true," replied her sisters.

So Lucinda and Arabella continued
to pamper Prince Ribbit.

They let him sleep in the
biggest, softest bed…

…and gave him the finest clothing
and a beautiful new crown.

Martha was the only person who saw
Prince Ribbit for what he really was.

"You may be clever, but you're just an ordinary frog!" she insisted.

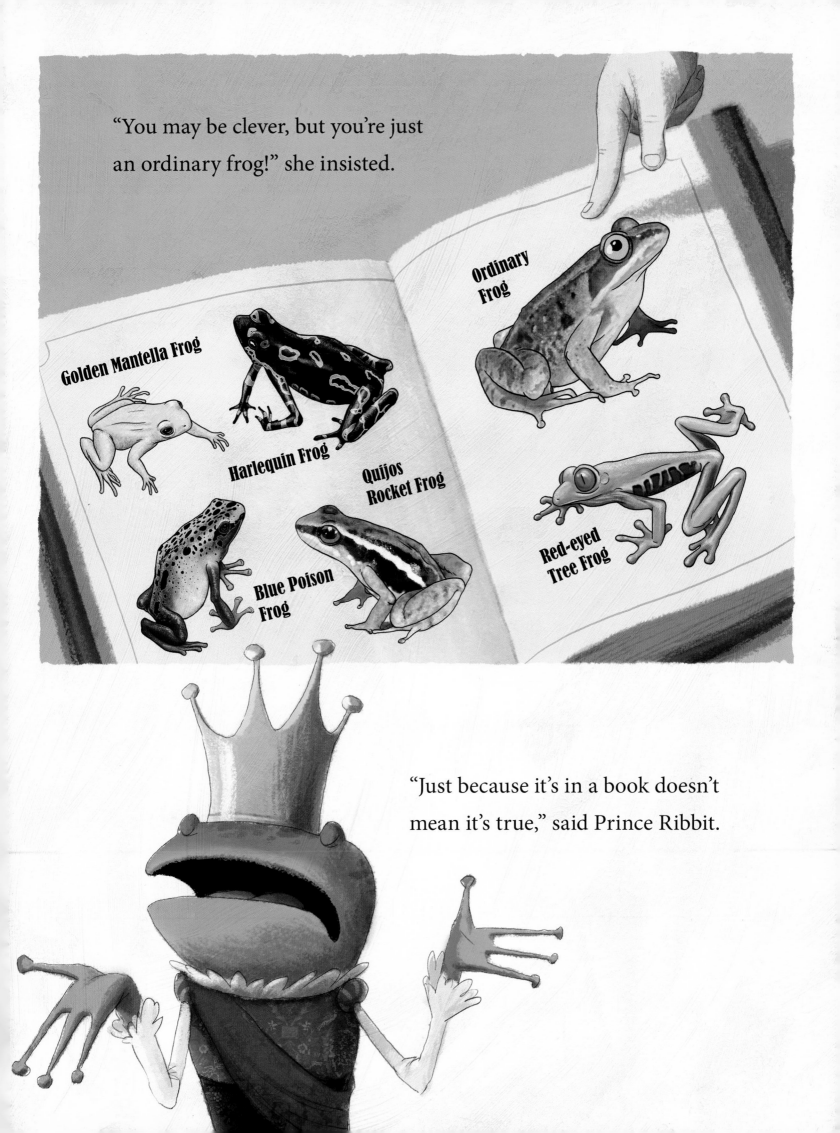

"Just because it's in a book doesn't mean it's true," said Prince Ribbit.

This is hopeless, thought Martha. *My sisters will never believe me, no matter how many books of facts I show them. But I suppose I'm just as stubborn. I've never read their storybooks. Perhaps I should…*

So Martha gathered a big pile of fairy tales and began to read.

She was surprised to find that, while the stories might not be true,
they were often funny, exciting, and inspiring.

And after Martha had read them all, she
knew exactly what to do with Prince Ribbit.

"If you're really an enchanted prince, why hasn't the spell been broken yet?" Martha asked Prince Ribbit the next morning.

Prince Ribbit shifted uneasily in his little golden throne and adjusted his little golden crown.

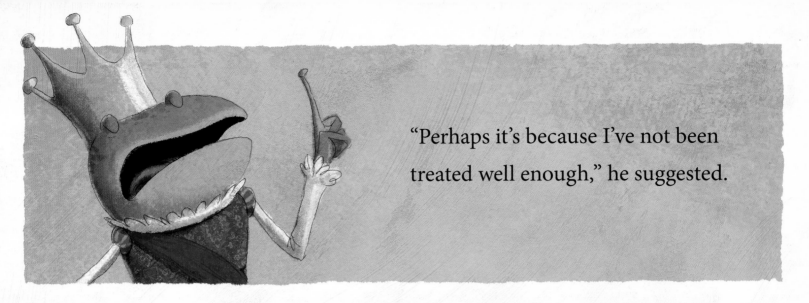

"Perhaps it's because I've not been treated well enough," he suggested.

"You seem very well treated to me!" said Martha. "I think it's time to try something different. What's the one thing that will always break an evil spell?"

"TRUE LOVE'S KISS!"

cried Arabella and Lucinda.

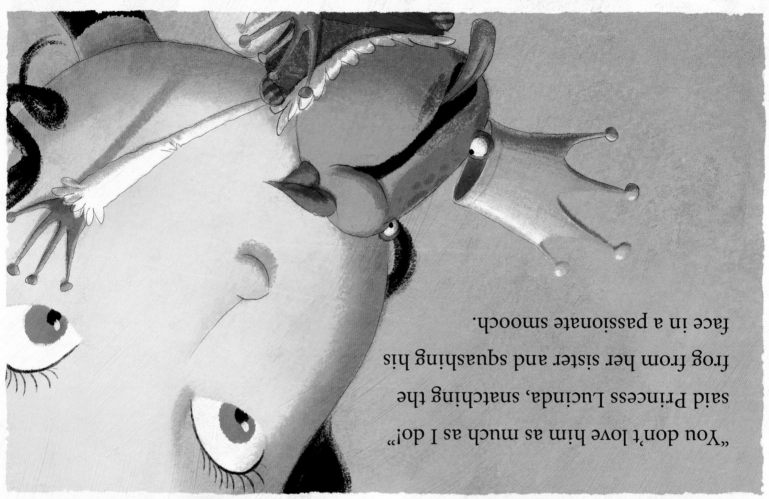

"You don't love him as much as I do!" said Princess Lucinda, snatching the frog from her sister and squashing his face in a passionate smooch.

"Me first," said Arabella, planting a big wet smacker on Prince Ribbit's clammy cheek.

But no matter how many kisses they gave him, Prince Ribbit remained very much a frog. And, in the end, both princesses realized that this was all he'd ever been and all he'd ever be.

"I suppose I should go back to my pond," sighed the frog,
taking off his beautiful crown. But he looked so sad that
Martha couldn't help feeling sorry for him.

"Please don't go," she said. "Any animal smart enough to fool my sisters would be fun to have around. And while I might not want a handsome prince as a husband, I'd LOVE to have a clever frog as a friend!"

She picked up the frog and gave him a gentle kiss.

The instant Martha kissed him, a huge puff of pink smoke appeared, and the frog turned into a handsome young prince.

In fact, he was SO handsome that Martha decided that she DID want to marry him after all. So she fell into his arms, and they both lived happily ever after!